I0634816

913 000 00097945

For Jamil and Quinn, with love.
D.A.

To my mum and dad
who always encouraged me to be an artist.
P.C.

CHOICES CHOICES
TAMARIND BOOKS 9781870516839

Published in Great Britain by Tamarind Books,
a division of Random House Children's Books
A Random House Group Company

This edition published 2007
Reprinted 2009

3 5 7 9 10 8 6 4 2

Text copyright © Dawne Allette, 2007
Illustrations copyright © Paul Cemmick, 2007

Set in Stanley

TAMARIND BOOKS
61–63 Uxbridge Road, London, W5 5SA

www.tamarindbooks.co.uk
www.kidsatrandomhouse.co.uk

Addresses for companies within The Random House Group Limited can be found at: www.randomhouse.co.uk/offices.htm

THE RANDOM HOUSE GROUP Limited Reg. No. 954009

A CIP catalogue record for this book is available from the British Library.

Printed and bound in Singapore

Choices, choices...

Dawne Allette
illustrated by Paul Cemmick

Tamarind

What will I be when I am a man? It is never too early to start making a plan.

I have thought and thought about what I should do... I will be an explorer in Katmandu.

I like riding horses.

I love racing cars.

It is not easy picking and choosing.

A runner...

or a swimmer?

I love to eat
and I love
to cook.

I will be a food critic
with a best-selling book.

a bricklayer or painter.

I will be a chemist
with wild, crazy hair.

Or a clothing designer for
Little Boys' Wear.

I will paint or take pictures of landscapes around us...

be an actor
or director,

or a clown
in the circus.

I will write books
for children
about animals
and birds,

be a school teacher
sharing new words.

I have so many ideas
buzzing round
in my head.

Tomorrow
I will choose
Now I am going
to bed!

OTHER TAMARIND TITLES

FOR *Choices, Choices* READERS
What Will I Be?
Danny's Adventure Bus
Siddharth and Rinki
Big Eyes, Scary Voice
Caribbean Animals
South African Animals
All My Friends
A Safe Place
The Night the Lights Went Out
Time for Bed
Time to Get Up
Dave and the Tooth Fairy
Giant Hiccups

BOOKS FOR WHEN YOU GET A LITTLE OLDER…
Amina and the Shell
The Dragon Kite
Mum's Late
Marty Monster
The Bush
The Feather
Princess Katrina and the Hair Charmer
Boots for a Bridesmaid
Starlight
Yohance and the Dinosaurs

FOR BABIES
Baby Goes
Baby Noises
Baby Finds
Baby Plays

FOR TODDLERS
Let's Have Fun
Let's Go to Playgroup
Let's Feed the Ducks
Let's Go to Bed

And if you are interested in seeing the rest of
our list, please visit our website:
www.tamarindbooks.co.uk